H. Clay Wright

Burlesque Statesmanship

Or, the Gubernatorial-Senatorial-Editorial-Conclavorial-Fizzleatorial Coup

d'état.

H. Clay Wright

Burlesque Statesmanship
Or, the Gubernatorial-Senatorial-Editorial-Conclavorial-Fizzleatorial Coup d'état.

ISBN/EAN: 9783337123277

Printed in Europe, USA, Canada, Australia, Japan

Cover: Foto ©Andreas Hilbeck / pixelio.de

More available books at **www.hansebooks.com**

BURLESQUE STATESMANSHIP:

OR,

The Gubernatorial-Senatorial-Editorial Conclavorial-Fizzleatorial Coup D' Etat.

A Melo-Dramatic, Comico-Tragico-Burlesque

IN FIVE ACTS.

BY H. CLAY WRIGHT.

——"O, but man—proud man!
Drest in a little brief authority,
Cuts such fantastic tricks before high heaven
As make the angels weep."—*Shakspeare.*
"Rust, sword! cool blushes and Delgrado live.
Safest in shame!"—*Ibid.*

LEAVENWORTH, KANSAS:
PRINTED AT THE CONSERVATIVE JOB OFFICE.
1861.

To D. W. WILDER, ESQ.

As a slight token of my esteem for him as a gentleman, a scholar, an able and earnest writer, and a fearless advocate of the true principles of self-government and the rights of human nature, this Hudibrastic effusion is respectfully inscribed by his unworthy but earnest co-laborer and ever faithful friend,

H. CLAY WRIGHT.

PROLOGUE.

From ancient to the latest hour of time,
Since man first learned to clothe his thoughts in rhyme.
Each subtle plot by daring author hurl'd,
To run the gantlet of the critic world,
(Where every note—by keen-edged poinard met.
By literary wolves and bears beset,—
Must pay a tribute to the hungry brood,
Whose stock of knowledge and whose mental food
Are garnered up in wiser people's domes
To be dealt out in less or longer tomes,
Just as the doctor doles his cure-all pills,
That curing one create a thousand ills,)
In reasons corselet must be trebly steeled
To run successful 'round the epic field;
For lacking this, 'tis labor misemployed,
Of every worth and usefulness devoid:
A paper wad fired off with thundering sound,
Which, wanting weight, falls harmless to the ground

Should any ask what reason here is shown,
Or where the purpose that these pages own,
To such we say, Go scan each sentence well,
On every line with mark'd attention dwell,
And judge the whole not by its lack of wit,
Which, while it pleases, is but counterfeit.
For lo! no phantom beings figure here
With voice and mien to please the eye and ear.
But these are men well known to public fame,
Whose acts shall speak their honor or their shame;
For men by acts and not by words are weighed—
No words can cure what actions have betrayed:
Even as the deadly fruit upon the tree
May feed the eye with boundless ecstacy;

And, while untouched upon the stem it hangs,
Its velvet rind may hide its serpent fangs;
But plucked and wounded, lo! the pulp beneath
Leaps like a deadly poinard from its sheath,
And scatters woe where we had looked for bliss.—
That hidden 'neath the velvet cloak of this,—
So Virtue's mantle often covers Vice,
So eloquence oft hides a base device.

The golden scabbard, set with diamonds bright,
That dazzle with their variegated light,
Tells not the temper of the blade it hides,
The deadly tenant that within abides;
But we, enraptured with the scabbard's blaze,
Forget the weapon as on this we gaze;
So words well chosen fascinate the ear,
Dispel each doubt and neutralize each fear,
Till we, like Eve in Eden's ancient bowers,
Submissive bow, and own their serpent power.

No falsehoods in these pages congregate,
Nor have we written with the pen of hate,
Beyond that hatred fierce of vice and crime,
That fires the poet to indignant rhyme,
That blazes on the patriot's 'venging blade,
Who mourns the while he dons war's direful trade,
And call'd by duty to the gory field,
Throws by his hatred when his foeman yield.
So we, a stranger to the poet's fire,
Hurl not the poet's but the patriot's ire;
Invoking not the muse of idle dreams
But only seeking to unmask the schemes
Of a detested, politican race,
Who are to manhood's name a foul disgrace;
Whose lives evince them but a living lie,
Unfit to live and twice unfit to die!

Behold our country, bleeding rent and torn;
Our institutions of their glory shorn;
Behold our land by treason's host o'er run;
Go on our battlefields and witness there
The foul and damning deeds his hand hath done;
The shriek, the groan, the ravings of despair,
The curse, the wail, the supplicating prayer,
Of bleeding hosts cut down forever, and undone,—
Proud Freedom's banner trampled in the dust!

Ask you the cause? Power's damn'd and hateful lust—
That dagger hidden 'neath a patriot mien—
Which stabs more surely as it stabs unseen!
That curse Ambition, Freedom's deadly foe,
Which flatters while it seeks to overthrow;
Armed with sweet words, in righteous robes arrayed—
An angel's garb dorn'd for a devil's trade.

If, for the sake of unity of plot,
Some scenes are here in truth enacted not,
Yet shall the living characters confess
We have not clothed them in a borrowed dress;
For he who hides deceit 'neath Virtue's pall,
Damn'd in great crimes, is surely damn'd in small.
And we, who know his major crimes full well,
May guess that heaven no consort makes with hell.
Can love and hatred round one heart entwine?
Can crime and virtue in one breast combine?
Then is the devil worthy double paint—
A blacker devil and a whiter saint!

    *   *   *   *   *

If Monsieur Croaker is dissatisfied,
And thinks we have some pregnant facts denied;
If Petti-brain is sorry we have not
A female woman in our little plot;
If Pedigree is anxious 'bout our sire,
Or Steeple that we worship 'neath his spire;
If Ballotbox would like to make a note
For whom and how we last "put in" our vote,
If Policy—dear tender-hearted sleek—
Grieves that we're not a favorite with his clique;
If Mutual Admiration—flush with smiles—
Would tickle us, but fears our depth of wiles,
And hides his cat's tail in its golden urn,
For fear we would not tickle in return;
We here return our compliments to all,
But promise none, not willing to forestall
Our unrestricted right, with hand and mind,
To labor for the good of all mankind;
And as we others judge by their own deeds,
We rest on ours—contented with their meeds,
And answer those who many points inquire—
We are a man—so was our great-grandsire;
And, if we are not sadly misinformed,
Our mother was a woman—woman formed.

Ye critics, born of Jove's almighty brain,
Who shake your lightnings o'er the epic plain,
Reserve your deadly shafts for wiser men,
We are unworthy of your scathing pen ;
We claim no place with literary gods,
Nor shall we tremble when a critic nods;
Nor dread of censure, nor the hope of praise,
Hath spur'd or lured the spirit of our lays ;
We seek no favor, fear no foeman's hate,
Shall strive—what ere may be our future fate—
To act our part, without an "if we can,"
To do our duty as becomes a man,
Well knowing that, in this, our sordid clod
Becomes the grandest poetry of God.

        *   *   *   *   *

Rouse, sons heroic of heroic sires,
And "light anew" your fathers' beacon fires !
Ye men whose hands are scarred with honest toil,
Ye are the guardians of our sacred soil ;
On ye our country's destiny is placed,
Her honor stain'd, your mem'ry is disgraced.
Her laws kept pure, with fervent glow sublime,
Your names shall beam adown the path of time.
And Freedom, in countless ages hence.
Shall bless the men who stood in her defence.

Then rise and shield her in this trying hour,
When fraud and bribery would destroy her power,
When low-brow'd vice, with money at command,
Plays with a skilful, parricidal hand ;
When honesty his sceptre hath resigned,
And polished rogues are gentlemen refined :
When asses asses buy for yellow gold,
And *men* are by *official asses* sold ;
Rise in your might, and show these dastard slaves
How swift they've dug their own dishonor'd graves.
Rise, prove ye're men " who know, and dare maintain"
Your sacred rights—on land or ocean main.
Rise, hurl corruption from the halls of State—
And earn the title of the truly great.

Burlesque Statesmanship.

ACT I.

Scene 1.—*Leavenworth—St. Thomas Discovered Sipping his Wine.*

St. Thomas (soliloquizing.)

Could I go up but just another grade,
Is still the cry when the last round's been made.
Up, up— still up! and none will be content
With what he is—he who is President
Would *be* a *King;* the King would wage a war,
Could he but gain *one* step—*excelsior.*
That word lends hope to man's expiring breath,
And lights him o'er the gloomy vale of death ;
Sits where he sleeps, in earth's sepulchral clod ;
Points mortal to immortal, earth to God !
The school-boy, pondering o'er his irksome task,
Fires, as he hopes in college halls to bask ;
The student now—another wish is there—
He longs to sit in the *Professor's* chair.
And thus, still up—ambition knows no pause ;
Excelsior still gleams, still lures, still draws,
Still on ahead, nor casts one look behind—
The bane, the curse, the ruin of mankind !
No matter now, the thing I *am* is naught—
To be much *more* shall lend its wings to thought,
And thought to deed, till *I be what I ought !*
I would be Senator—aye, would and *must*—
Will be !—tho' I usurp the sacred trust !

But how?—that cursed Lane!—had it a turn.
The place for which I sigh, for which I burn.
Were mine, indeed. 'Tis quite too much for me—
I fear to rouse the people's jealousy.

Enter FITZPOODLE-HINDOO, FAITHFUL TRAY, TIMES *and* JO-
HANNESVONFREELINGHUYSENSOURCROUTSENEINDITENSTRAUT-
ZENBERGER ZEITUNG.

Good morrow, sirs—how is it with you, friends?
Is aught conceived that to our purpose tends?
Say, shall I realize my august dreams?
Come, drink some wine—and then divulge your scheme.

Johannes-von-Zeitung.

Mein noble lort unt master, great unt vise,
Ve vished to make you leetle bit surprise;
Ve've got von grandest plan, und ver' moch more—
Ich never vas so petter as goot pefore—
'Tis monish—dat ish all ve vant to vin:
Yust push te rhino, und ve'll catch dem in.
You bay us each von tousand dollar piece—
Ve'll do your vork, und must have pread und cheese.
Und den de members must be bought, you know.
Und dat ish all—und higher up you go.

Fitz-Hindoo.

Yes, sir; that is our plan: if you will bleed.
We pledge our honor that you shall succeed.
The road to *honor* is a thorny way,
But if you have the wherewithal to pay,
If you will grasp at once the fleeting hour.
Smooth is the road, and broad and short to power.

Faith. Times.

This is your only chance: if you would win,
You must come down with plenty of the tin;
To each of us a thousand dollars give,
. For we must have the wherewithal to live;)
And when you have the place and all is sure.
Positions good for us you must secure.

Saint Thomas.

Your plan is good: I like it passing well,
And words would fail my gratitude to tell.
And should dame Fortune lift me to the skies,
You shall be sharers in her gifts likewise.
But should we fail the Press to subsidize—

Johannes von Zeitung.

Fear not. mein lort; yust find the perquisites
We'll see you haf enough of parasites,
Ich can puy up de Yarmans mit your dimes.
De Copperheads vill nibble at de *Dimes,*
Und Brudder Hindoo, mit his trembling lyre (liar)
Will make your victory all you can desire.

Saint Thomas.

Still, still I fear to disobey the laws,
And link my name with a detested cause:
I would be great, but would thro' virtue win—
I dread the power that comes through moral sin

Faith. Times.

Since vice is virtue by the laws of hell.
There is no spot where virtue may not dwell:
What is a crime when first the thing's begun.
May prove a virtue when the act is done.
Since Proudhon lore makes every good a crime.
And Satan. God—a rogue is always prime.

Fitz-Hindoo.

Successful treason's honored in the laws ;
A crime at birth—its end a holy cause:
Had Arnold but succeeded in his scheme—
Of many a lay his name had been the theme—
And WASHINGTON had been a traitor. knave.
Unwept, unsung, in foul dishonor's grave.
Had Satan been successful in the strife
That aimed a blow at his Creator's life,
The universe had trembled at his nod.
And own'd him sovereign—universal God.

Johan. Von Zeitung.

What tho' the serpent marr'd Eve's Eden-life.
And stained the honor of a loving wife:
What tho' he 'complished Adam's foul disgrace.
And entailed horrors on the human race.
May not his wisdom fire the poet's lays,
Inspire the lute to warble in his praise?
And you. mein lort, shall lack no parasite
Your virtues rare in sterling verse to write.

Saint Thomas.

Enough ! We'll go to yonder secret room.
And there our incantations will resume.

In Richard's words, "lets on pell mell—
If not to heaven, why, hand-in-hand to hell!"

[*Exeunt omnes*

SCENE II.—*Ante chamber—Dark—Cauldron in center.*

Enter ST. THOMAS, FITZ HINDOO, FAITH. TIMES *and* JOHAN
VON ZEITUNG.

Saint Thomas.

Sprites that rule the vasty deep,
And o'er hell your vigils keep,
Break the bands of Lethean thrall,
Cleave the dun and sulphurous pall,
Spread your wings and hie to earth,
Aid us in a monstrous birth;
We've conceived it—child of hell—
And invoke your magic spell,
Or it may ne'er greet our sight—
Haste and woo it to the light!
Here are charms of human gore,
Shed on Dixie's crimson shore,
Sighs that I have heaved for years
Vial of politician's tears :   [*Throws them in Cauldron.*
In the seething cauldron bubble,
And relieve me of my trouble.   [*Stirs Cauldron*

Fitz Hindoo.

Charms are here of rarest worth :
Virtue strangled at its birth,
Ere I came to man's estate :
Hair from Jim Buchanan's pate;
Horned toad from Jim Lane's farm ;
Blood from Cleveland red and warm,
These the ingredients rich and rare,—[*Throws them in.*
Leave us not in dire dispair !   [*Stirs Cauldron.*

Faith. Times.

Venom of a Copperhead ;
Tears by Burrel Taylor shed ;
Type that stamp'd that fatal page,
Mover of the people's rage;
Pot-house songs and ribald jests;
Virtue from a harlot pressed.   [*Throws them in.*

Johan. Von Zeitung.

Ich hab no mooch to gib at all,
Ich gib mein character unt all :

Its sphotted, sthriped; not mooch white,
Unt ver' much blacker dan de night.   [*Throws it in*

          [*All stir, and sing.*
Stir the cauldron—while it boils
We may scent the coming spoils;
Lo, it has a brimstone smell,
See, he comes—the child of hell.   [*Spirit rises.*

                    Spirit.
Thomas, Thomas, Thomas; beware Jim Lane—
"Great God," beware—he is a wicked Thane:
Put him away and thou may'st laugh to scorn
The blows of any politician born.   [*Spirit descends.*

                 Saint Thomas.
Thou'st harp'd my fears aright! And now we'll go
And send him kiting to the shades below.
Come tortures thick and fast as pattering rain,
The earth shall know I have not lived in vain.
                              [*Exeunt omnes.*

      SCENE III.—*Topeka—St. Thomas Discovered.*
                 Saint Thomas.
Thus far thro' foam cap'd billows have we steered
Before the gale; nor wind has lull'd nor veered;   ·
My friends have worked with an unwavering will.
My subsidies full many a coffer fill;
And now I rise majestic—glorious—great!
Chief genius 'mong the genii of State.
What subterfuges, tricks I have suborned,
In pregnant plea to have my rival scorned.
And am I worse than he—the lank, grim chief?
And is a liar worse than is a thief?
I lie to get the place he would retain;
He steals in hopes to get it back again;
I slander him with lies by others made;
He steals the bolts for which my money paid,
Repolishes and hurls them back on me,
And makes me squirm 'neath stolen repartee.
Had I a bolt of hot consuming fire,
Or could I buy up some renowned liar,
Some literary god, some *bel esprit*,
Who'd wound him sore with many *jeu d' esprit*;
Yes, that's the thing—these papers that I've bought
Too often in their own vile traps are caught;
Their lies are shallow, flimsy, silly, bare—

Some one I'll have who's cute at splitting hair.
I'll get the place—of that I am apprised—
But how to keep it I have not devised:
The people must have reasons, thus and so,
Unless you give them—overboard you go.
Who are the people, that they should inspire
The fear to rouse their virtue's latent ire?
They're apish dolts with overweening pride—
The asses that the knaves of fortune ride.

[*Enter Johan. Von Zeitung.*

Johan. Von Zeitung.

Mein Gott in heimel! here's von tam lampoon
Vich say de lion's skin infolds a coon,
Dat *you* be's von *genus* mit hybrid paw,
Unt (Ich nix feestay,) *bon chat a bon rat.*
Ich ax vat vas de meaning of dat vord;
A man he say, " vat, have you never heard?"
Unt den he laugh unt say it means a mule,
Unt say it meant *you* vas von piggest fool.

Saint Thomas.—(*Majestically.*)

A trick—a scheme to thwart me, that is plain!
A sickly flower cull'd from a sickly brain.
We'll rise above the foe's low flung abuse,
And show him that his sharpest wit's obtuse.

[*Enter Fitz-Hindoo in haste.*

Fitz-Hindoo.

Should I report what I have seen and heard,
Your veins would swell to bursting at a word:
Your heart would snap its tendons with surprise:
Forth from their sockets leap your glaring eyes,
And every muscle tremble in your frame,
To know that man is so devoid of shame.

Saint Thomas.—(*In towering grandeur.*)

Think'st thou *I* care? am *I* not mail'd and steel'd?
Think'st thou *I* fear the ghosts of Bosworth field?
Think'st thou *I* dread to meet the hosts of Lane?
I'll force them back unto their lair again!
Why art thou pale? Why tremblest in thy shoes?
Art thou white livered? Speak, and tell thy news.

[*Exit Johan. Zeitung.*

Fitz-Hindoo.

Great sir, as I was passing from my room
My work important that I might resume,

And meditating as I shut the door,
This paper fell before me on the floor;
From whence it came, or how, I do not know,
But fear it is a summons from below;
At least it says you must prepare to go!
[*Reads.*]—It says: "Fitz-Hindoo, you should be more wise.
Nor trust the sight of thy delusive eyes;
For crabbed age may pass for genial youth,
A lie well garnished pass for sterling truth;—
Prepare a coffin free from stain or paint,
Your master soon will be a defunct saint."

[*Enter Faith. Tray Times, much agitated.*

Faith. *Tray Times.*
O woe is me! that I should see the day?

Saint Thomas.
Out, craven-hearted—take thy face away!
I am prepared to brave the frowns of fate,
And bid defiance to black-hearted hate!

[*Exit Eitz-Hindoo.*

I'll sink in splendor, if I sink at all,
And the whole earth shall tremble when I fall;
And, when I yield to hate's infernal stroke,
My funeral pyre shall send up amber smoke!
Speak out! If evil lurks athwart our path,
We'll boldly meet and smite it in our wrath!

Faith. *Tray Times.*
Last night as I retired unto my bed,
A whirling lightness capered through my head;
The excitement I have endured so long,
Played on my nerves a little bit too strong.
I could not sleep—my mind was in deep gloom,
And spirits seemed to hover in the room;
The clock struck twelve—I started in affright,
Quick threw the covers off, and—sat upright!

Saint Thomas.
What did'st thou see? some goblin damn'd and grim?
The counter-type of lean and haggard Jim!

Faith. *Tray Times.*
Close by my bed a fierce, wild demon stands
With blood red eyes, and white and bony hands;
I could not stir; my flesh was dead and chill;
My hair stood up, my heart and pulse were still.

Saint Thomas.

Oh! this is very ecstacy of woe!
Had he no kindly message to bestow?
Methinks I see him now—did he not speak?
What was he like? A sunken, palid cheek?
A god-like brow? A towering stately mien?
A mellow voice? A dignity serene?

Faith. Tray Times.

With solemn intonations full and round,
His voice a hollow and sepulchral sound,
His cold and clammy hand was raised on high,
And fiery flames kept darting from his eye:
"Be not deceived," he said, "by outward looks;—
If only facts were printed in the books,
The world would be a changed world indeed,
And man would seem a vastly different breed.
The wily statesman may deceive the mass,
May *seem* a god, yet *be* an arrant ass;
"Statesman" is linked to many a sorry knave,
Who stabs the country he pretends to save.
The politician, too, with studied grace,
With candied tongue and smooth angelic face,
With rounded periods sounding very nice,
Oft holds his honor at a paltry price;
He's but a rascal, when the truth is told,
Who'd barter country for a sum of gold:
But man and master soon will be found out,
And saint and sinner shall be put to rout."

Saint Thomas.

'Tis not at me the weak satire is aimed,—
What man has *bought* right justly may be claimed,
The place I've bought—and paid for mighty well;
Nor have I bought with an intent to sell.
Go send him back to languish and repine,
Where he belongs,—what I have bought is mine!
I am no fool——

Faith. Tray Times.

But, yet, alas! too fond:
You do mistake the tenor of the bond—
"A pound of flesh—of blood no single drop;"
Or, "*when* the people bid proceedings stop"—

Saint Thomas.

I understand; their voice must be obeyed—
You're merely pledged to lend me all your aid.

Faith. Tray Times.
That is the tenor of the bond, your grace;
And I am bound that you shall have the place;
When you have got it, make it firm and sure.

Saint Thomas.
O, never fear, I'll hold it quite secure;
All pleas I'll mock, all threats I'll laugh to scorn,
"Brandished by man that's of a woman born!"

[*Enter Johan Von Zeitung, hastily.*

Johan. Von Zeitung.
Vat, ho! mein lort, Sid. Clarke is on de seas:

Saint Thomas.
Then be the seas on him! Down on thy knees,
Thou lily-livered boy! Stop, while I think,
We'll go to Blake's and take another drink.
And in the words of Iago, "hell and night
Must bring this monstrous birth to the world's light.

[*Exeunt omnes.*

ACT II.

SCENE I.—*Topeka—Bar Room, Lobby Members, Blowers and Strikers, smoking, drinking, et cetera.*

Enter SAINT THOMAS, FAITHFUL TRAY TIMES *and* JOHAN. VON ZEITUNG.

Saint Thomas.
Come, drink, my friends; there's joy in sparkling wine—
Then drink, and praise the virtue of the vine;
For friendship's ties are strengthened as we drain
The foaming juice; a rapture fills each vein.
Yes, there is power in wine and woman's love,
That lifts the soul all vulgar themes above;
Then drink, my friends, let rapture fill each breast:
Pledge, pledge the toast, and crack the cutting jest.

[While they are drinking, a religious member of the Legislature takes Von Zeitung aside and insinuates that St. Tom will be expected to deliver a moral lecture over and above financial perquisites. Von Zeitung "under-

stands his biz," and gives the Saint the cue, and offers
him an original M. S. Poor Tom can't see it. He un-
derstands Greek, but is utterly illiterate in the " Yarman
alphabet." Faithful Tray Times sees the dilemma, and
kindly rushes forward with his M. S. on the Millenium.]

Saint Thomas, (*reading M. S.*)
" What tho' the serpent—cursed 'bove every beast—
Be doomed in dust to crawl, on dust to feast;
What though proud Reason's placed beyond his reach.
And he hath lost his thrilling powers of speech ;
These to his snakeship shall again return,
And in his breast with tenfold fervor burn.
Know, every creature was, by Adam's fall.
Bereft of speech, enchained in instincts thrall ;
Not that the creature in itself had erred,
But man was fore-ordained to be preferred,
And wisdom could not break Almighty's laws,
Though tender love plead hard their injured cause:
These, for the time shall sigh and groan in pain.
But they shall have their liberty again :
Omnific wisdom hath devised the plan
To *save* the Creature and *redeem* the Man.
Both man and beast shall have a common speech.
And dwell in love and amity with each :
The leopard, lion, fatling, calf and kid,
Shall go where'er a little child may bid ;
Nor man, nor beast, shall feel the least alarm ;
The serpent shall forget his power to harm ;
The sucking child shall play within his nest,
The weaned child shall seek his den to rest :
The earth her pristine vigor shall assume,
The dreary waste with flowers eterne shall bloom.
Where now the thistle mocks man's weary toil,
Rich fruits shall spring spontaneous from the soil.

[Loud and prolonged cheers. Religious gentleman is
glad to see that the Saint is orthodox, and invites the
crowd to liquor up.]

[*Enter Fitz-Hindoo.*
Fitz-Hindoo, (*aside to Saint Tom.*)
The Legislative Mill has 'gan to run—
Each wants his toll before your grist's begun.

Saint Thomas, (*giving Hindoo bank check.*)
Here is the toll—bid them put me through :
I'll be as faithful to their interests, too.

[*Exit Fitz-Hindoo.*

Faith. Tray Times.
Live while you may; nor grief nor trouble borrow;
Spend what you have, and pray for more to-morrow.
[*They drink. Re-enter Hindoo.*
Fitz-Hindoo.

Whipped are your foes; our victory is complete,
And you shall sit in the Grim Chieftain's seat.
[*All shout.*
Song by Faith. Tray Times.
Jim Lane's carcass is laid upon the shelf,
And we'll have a chance to steal a little pelf;
I'll have a foreign mission to go upon, myself,
And bask in monarch's smiles.

Song by Fitz.Hindoo.
And I'll have a chance to run with the " masheen: "
I'll get a major's commission and sell it well, I ween,
For five hundred dollars! now you mustn't think I'm
green;
Ah ha! I am well matured.

Song by Johan. Von Zeitung.
Ich am von leetle tog, and I vears my master's collar;
He give me von pig office und von leetle tousand dollar
Yere's a Yarman up a gum-stump—don't you hear him
holler—
Zwei glass lager peer!
[*They execute a witches dance, and scene closes.*

Scene II.—*Private office of Saint Thomas—Dark—Lucifer
dimly seen on one side of desk.*

Enter Saint Thomas (*who has been out holding a jubilee with
his confreres,) and takes seat on the other side.*

Saint Thomas (musing.)
'Tis an awful night; what a dreadful storm;
My blood is freezing.

Lucifer (aside.)
—I could make it warm.
I'm here, my boy, just in the nick of time;
I wonder how he'd like a warmer clime?

Saint Thomas.
I'm shivering, yet on fire! That cursed club,
To keep me out so late.

Lucifer (aside.)
Aye, there's the rub—
He would be great, and so, perforce, must be
Suaviter in modo, fortiter in re !

Saint Thomas.
But then, if I their Senator would be,
Why, I must court their favor for the time—
Till I am firmly seated.

Lucifer (aside.)
Well, that's prime.
He'd be a dangerous fellow down below,
His cunning schemes might play the deuce, you know.

Saint Thomas.
Our ship's cut loose and drifting in the storm !

Lucifer (aside.)
Be careful, boy ; it might become too warm
For pleasant sailing.

Saint Thomas.
I must mount the deck—

Lucifer (aside.)
And should your scow become a total wreck ?

Saint Thomas.
Once mounted, where I'll stop, 'tis hard to tell !

Lucifer (aside.)
Just on the confines of the lowest—well !

Saint Thomas.
'Tis well we do not know what is to be.

Lucifer (aside)
Accursed is he that hangeth on a tree.

Saint Thomas.
O that a laurel wreath my head may deck,
And Honor's chain be girdled round my neck !

Lucifer (aside)
Yes ; when you get a little lower down,
Your brows shall glitter with a brimstone crown—
A bright tiara seal your princely hope,
And you shall be of my domains the Pope.

Saint Thomas.
But, then, I shrink from what I've done.   What dread
Comes o'er me !—in the abodes of the dead—

The silent, gloomy chambers of the earth —
Is all repose ? Or does grim death give birth
To other life ? Shall hope and life become
Alike extinct ? Is death the total sum
Of all existence ? Oh ! is there not some spot—
A period whence all things are forgot?
A time when sorrow's anxious, aching breast
Shall be in peace ?

Lucifer (aside.)

Where rascals are at rest
He means. Yes, Thomas ; thou shalt find that place
And live a life where crime is no disgrace.
Should he indulge in usurpation schemes,
I'll read him Greely on Utopian dreams :
I'll have my laws made stronger on that point—
My bishopric he might put out of joint;
Pluck off my kingly coronet from my head,
Usurp my throne, and leave me nary red.

Saint Thomas.

Why, in the list of crimes mine's not the <i>first</i>,
Nor will it be the last or very <i>worst</i>.
The best of men has kingly David been—
And yet his reign was tinged with mortal sin ;
With crimes that shock the finer sense of right,
And bury virtue in perennial night.
A murdered husband and dishonored wife
Attest <i>his</i> virtue and his holy life.
And Solomon, the wisest of the earth—
His wisdom, sure, was very little worth ;
It wrote him highest on the scroll of fame,
And blacker dyed the records of his shame.
If these, anointed by God's holy hand,
Spread want and famine o'er a thrifty land,
Shall, then, the deeds of those more brightly shine,
Who lay no claim to rule by right divine ?—
A woman's charms may cause a <i>Saint</i> to sin.

Lucifer (aside.)

Yes ; handsome Eve once took me sadly in ;
That scrape with her gave me a stunning blow ;
And woman—hum !—their company I forego
Now, he's in love—that's plain as A, B, C—
And rankling sore with mortal jealousy ;
No doubt been jilted by some damsel fair,
With killing eyes that smite him to despair

I wonder how he'd trade her off for mine—
I'm getting somewhat tired of Proserpine.

Saint Thomas.

Where are my friends that were to multiply
Like yonder stars, that stud the azure sky?
I look around—I cannot see a friend!
No; no!—not one on whom I can depend.
Oh! what a fool I am—a living lie!—
Did I not know esteem no gold can buy?
'Tis better to be honest and unknown,
Than to be flattered for your gold alone.
Do thou do right, tho' scorners may deride;
Stand by the truth—no evil shall betide;
For peace and safety are on Justice's side.
A *righteous* action is a source of joy,
And frees our pleasures from all base alloy—
A vestal fire that purifies the mind,
As crude gold melted issues forth refined;
But every *wrong* committed is a stain
That mars each pleasure, smothers joy with pain:
Steals like a nightmare o'er the guilty soul—
Or like the venom nestling in the bowl,
Which lures its victim with its balmy fumes,
And thrills his life-blood while to death it dooms.
Each virtue foster and each vice subdue;
Perform in haste what duty bids you do—
For duty and advantage are akin—
That well performed will surely this one win.
'Tis plainly written in great Nature's laws—
There's no effect but owns a parent cause:
A wicked act springs from a corrupt heart,
As impure fountains mucky streams impart—
A loathsome poison planted in the brain,
With lightning speed will course each swelling vein,
And though we think it hidden from the sight,
The blood will force it to the living light.
The wicked thoughts, which we would have concealed,
Are by our actions oftentimes revealed.
And men will stare with wonder and surprise,
To see how shallow has been our disguise.
Truisms all, that rend my heart in twain
To what I was (but ne'er shall be again—
An honest man) they point with scathing scorn!—
O God! I am of every virtue shorn!
The target of the people's vengeful ire,
Where fools may carp, and hurl their base satire.

Lucifer (aside.)
How strong and full the milk of virtue flows
Within his breast. What sturdy, telling blows
He deals upon his own devoted head ;
Like one to Virtue's manor born and bred.
Now, years ago I bought this very ape,
And have his papers tied beneath my tape :
He has not seen me, true—he can *not* see—
But none the less, I am his destiny.
Some people think they never have been bought,
Because the trap's unseen in which they're caught ;
But none the less, I own their sordid souls,
And hold their action 'neath my stern control.
And Tom is but the tool of my designs,
Bound fast to him his tongue so oft maligns,
He will repent, and in repenting sin ;
And while he does deplore, he hopes the act will win.
They talk of harps that have a thousand strings,
But he *ten* thousand variations sings ;
I'll make a noise to draw his mind this way,
And give him other strings on which to play.

[*Air in room stirs*

Saint Thomas (very much frightened.)
That noise ! Some person must be in the room :
Speak out, or meet thy everlasting doom.

[*Draws his pistol*

Speak out, I say, or die !—You see I'm armed.

Lucifer (aside.)
Saltpetre would'nt do me any harm.
(*Aloud*) Just save your powder, Tom, for mortal game,
You can't hurt *me*—I laugh at smoke and flame.

[*Thomas faints and scene closes.*

SCENE II.—*A fraudite bar-room—Faithful Tray Times, Fitz
Poodle Hindoo and Johannes Von Zeitung discovered.*

Johannes Von Zeitung.
Mein nople brooters vat is in de vind ?
You seem to be von veree much chagrin'd.
Ve've done our duty—all dat ve *could* do ;
Ve've vorked unt vorked—been faithful tried unt true :
Unt if de *beoples* vont pe caught mit chaff,
Ve should'nt cry like papies ven dey laugh.
Ve moosen't gif it up so soon—but vait
Unt catch dem mit anodder kind of bait,

Faith. Times.

True, true, my friend, our cause may seem quite lost,
And we like vessels wrecked and tempest toss'd,
But there is hope so long as life remains,
And if we fail, we're paid well for the pains.
I did not say the people would consent
(I could as well control the Pres dent,)
If he his office up to them will yield,
I'll break my sword and vanquished quit the field.
If he holds out, I'll be his faithful slave:
If he succumbs, why—I myself will save!
I've rode too long bestride of two extremes,
To be submerged 'neath any Phantom schemes.

Fitz-Hindoo.

I'm with you, sir; if he his cause will wreck,
I'll jump ashore before I break my neck :
And, like Delgrado, by my wit I'll thrive,—
" There's place and means for every man alive! "
[*Enter Saint Thomas, laboring under an aberration of mind.*
Good morrow, noble sir, you're wan and pale,
I hope your health has not begun to fail.

Saint Thomas (abstractedly.)

I am not well.   O, give me leave to go
Where I may hide me from the wary foe !

Johan. Von Zeitung.

Vy, how he speaks in an unnatural tone—
" O, vat a nople mind is here o'erthrown ! "

Saint Thomas (fiercely seizing Zeitung by the collar.)

If thou dost play me false, base hearted knave,
I'll hurl thee to a swift and bloody grave !
Where are the friends that you have promised me ?
Where is my money that you spent so free ?
Where are the bribes I paid to Church and State ?
The Legislature; people low and great ?
Have not I bought every low saloon ?
What am I called ?—A weak and silly loon !
Out upon ye ! swindlers, liars, slaves
To the lust of gain—infernal knaves!
       May woe betide the day—
The fatal day when first ye saw the light;
May it be blacker than the blackest night :
       May not a single ray
From Heaven's bright sun e'er pierce its sable gloom
Or gild the murky precincts of its tomb;

Blackened and blasted by your upas breath,
May it go down to everlasting death
Condemned with ye—dishonored and disgraced!
Out of my sight—ha! ha! ha! ha! away.

[*Falls in a swoon and is carried out on a shutter*

ACT III.

SCENE I.—*Times Office*—*Faithful Tray discovered.*
Faithful Tray Times.

Awake, O genius of my giant brain;
Thou goddess Thought, loud thro' thy fleshy fane,
Arouse the peals of thy immortal lyre,
And light thine altar with celestial fire;
I would, O Muse, in treach'rous schemes abound,
In subtle plots and cunning tricks profound.
O, shade of Shakspeare come! my thoughts inspire;
Imbue my mind with crafty Iago's fire.
I hate the Saint, as Iago did the Moor,
And second fiddle I will play no more:
I want the usurped office for myself;
Would be the *chief* dispenser of the pelf.
But how to sink Saint Thomas, deep in shame,
And raise *my* prospects by a double game!
My antecedents are so fully known,
I see no plan to give me proper tone,
Before the people's scrutinizing eyes;
And they may penetrate my thin disguise.
O, cursed fate! O, damned and hateful gold,
That lured me to his fatal cause uphold!
It is the cause: it is the fatal cause,
From which my plan its greatest trouble draws.
O! would that I had left his schemes alone,
And made myself more perfect in mine own!
But now to pull *him* from his high estate,
And claim *my* place among the proud and great!
I've been too bold, I've play'd my cards too strong,
To lure the people by my siren song;
My honesty the people won't believe,
And honest Iago can no more deceive.
What! I have never known such word as *fail*,
And by my sainted self I *will* prevail!

I'll have the office, sure—that's flat! But how?
Let's see! O happy thought! I have thee, now,
I'll show him his election's null and void.
And to resign it he may be decoy'd:
That 'tis illegal, in the law is plain,
And if he does resign, 'twill spare him pain ;
For, well I know, he ne'er can get the place—
Then I'll step in and save him from disgrace.
Thus, while I serve myself, I'll serve him, too:
And, thus, I am to mine own interest true.
But how can I the truth to him evince ?—
To contradict myself will make me wince !
I've told him it was legal, just and right ;
He'll scent the truth—and drive me from his sight.
'Tis plain I must approach him in disguise—
How shall I guard myself against surprise ?
I have it now—he's sick and sore at heart,
And I can easier play a double part.
Some elders of the church are stopping here
To fix their business for the coming year—
I'll visit Tom, and tell him it would be
A first-rate chance to show his charity,
And build his cause up with much greater ease,
Could he a little cash bestow on these.
That done, I will disguise myself, and come
As one of these, to thank him for his sum ;
And, in that guise, I'll coax him to resign :
Rise, rise! my soul! thou shalt in splendor shine!

[*Exit.*

SCENE II.—*Saint Thomas' office—St. Tom pacing back and
forth in a sad state of mind.*
Saint Thomas.

Out, damned spot! O, black and hateful stain !
That nought can cleanse and make me pure again !
So much for him who seeks to win *eclat*
At cost of every duty due to law.
What! coward conscience! why art thou dismay'd ?
I've broke no law—no duty disobey'd ?
Why should I fret and pine ? I should be gay !
The darker hour precedes the brighter day.
To-day, our honors bloom with fragrance fair ;
To-morrow, fade—and leave us bleak and bare !
To-day, our hopes run wanton to the sky ;
To-morrow, doomed to languish and to die.
And shall I, like a spaniel, whine and cower,
And yield to plebians my patrician power ?

No, no! 'Tis mine—it is mine honest due.
And I will hold it—dare, defy them, too!
[*Enter Faith. Tray Times.*
My noble friend—my honest, Faithful Tray :
When thou art gone all joys will flow away!

Faith. Tray Times.
You're merry, sir, to-day.

Saint Thomas.
Not I, my lord

Faith. Tray Times.
O, yes, you are ; you are, upon my word

Saint Thomas.
I love thee, sir, upon my life I do :
For I have seldom found a friend so true.
Here art thou, hearted, sir! [*strikes his breast.*] And here
    shall reign.
My most loved friend, till chaos comes again.

Faith. Tray Times.
My lord, I am unworthy such regard.

Saint Thomas.
Indeed, thou art my trump ; my winning card :
I've tried thee—and I hold thee passing well
In more respect than my poor words can tell.

Faith. Times.
I cry you quits, my noblest, best of friends :
But know not how to make your grace amends.
Thy generous kindness quite o'erwhelms me!

Saint Thomas.
My obligations are more due to thee.
I would that thou hads't power o'er my disease—
I must confess my mind is ill at ease.

Faith. Times
I'll tell thee what, my lord—don't think me rude—
Aside.)—'Tis an attack of moral turpitude—
(*Aloud.*)—'Tis moral phisic that thou most doth need,
Such as doth center in a noble need.
There are five Elders here ; and they do need
(For Elders on the things of earth do live.)
The little aid you can afford to give.
In giving them you do their aid secure.
And make your office firmer and more sure.

—4

Saint Thomas.

I did not think of that—it shall be done;
Here is a hundred dollars for each one;
Give each his share, and my respects to all.

Faith. Times (aside.)

Saint Thomas' greeting to his brother Paul.
(*Aloud.*)—I will, most worthy friend. Since we are in,
We'll bribe the church's goat to bear our sin. [*Exit*

Saint Thomas (looking after him admiringly.)

Now, by my faith, there goes an honest heart:
A friend from whom I would be loth to part. [*Exit*

SCENE III.—*St. Tom's office—St. Tom discovered.*

Saint Thomas.

'Tis now too late to pause; the deed is done,
The die is cast, and I the stake have won:
Shall I go back—blot out the hopes of years ?
To bend the knee, shed penitential tears?
Go back—the object of their scorn and hate?
Their taunts and jeers? No! I must brave my fate !

[*Enter Faith. T. Times, unseen by Tom, disguised as an Elder;
black wig, white neckerchief, green goggles, suit of "solemn" black,
black kids and umbrella.*]

Faith Times (aside.)

They say that everything is fair in war,
And rogues profound are men excelsior,
To win esteem is but to be discreet,
And honest *seem* to every man you meet.
Some men to act old Nick need no disguise;
I For he himself assumes a human guise;)
But he who would two devils deftly play,
Must *turn* his coat at least three times per day.
It is a sinking cause I have embraced,
And all who prop it up will be disgraced;
'Tis *bound* to fall—so I will haste its speed,
And place myself the hero in the lead :
I'll show myself a master rogue in this,
And Thomas' pain shall work me signal bliss.

Saint Thomas.

Repentance now cannot undo my crime,
But sink me lower down ; and for all time
My name would furnish food for ribald song
And jest, the by-word of the vulgar throng,
I must ahead, if I would win the game

On which I staked my honor, and my name!
But what's before me—death, or brighter fame ?
Undying honors, or unending shame?
Could I but penetrate the sable cloud
That veils the future in its mystic shroud ;
Could I but call the future from the tomb,
Would I, like Saul, rush on to certain doom ?
Yes, yes ; for me there is no pause nor turn !
Like yonder sun, I must mount up and burn ;
Must shed o'er earth an overpowering light,
Or sink, like Pleiad, in eternal night!
And yet, what consolation would it be,
Could I the end from the beginning see !
Aye, though my foul disgrace it did reveal,
Made blacker by each turn of Fortune's wheel,
Still I would wish to know the very worst,
To see the last as I have known the first !
O, that prescience on my sight would burst!
But no, it cannot be !

>*Faith. Tray Times (persuasively.)*
Indeed it can !
I'll hold thee up a glass, where thou may'st scan
The future at a glance ;—yes, thou may'st see
The good and bad that shall befall to thee.

>*Saint Thomas.*
Who art thou thus that break'st my reverie ?
A second Endor, come to blast my power,
And nip the bud ere it has 'gan to flower ?
Can'st thou unloose the sacred seals that bind
The future's page secure from finite mind,
Pierce the crude clay that shrouds my soul in night,
Cause ages hence to burst upon my sight ?
Here's money for thee—lift for me this pall,
And tell me whether I shall stand or fall.

>*Faith. Tray Times (aside.)*
He's bribed so much, his office and his bribes
Are all his thought ; just as the vulgar gibes
Of penny-a-liners—all their stock in trade,
Buoy up the author while they do degrade!
(*Aloud.*)—My dear Saint Thomas, I am much surprised.
I do not peddle necromantic lies.
I am beholden for your generous aid
And came to know how it may be repaid.

Saint Thomas.

An Elder? ha!

Faith. Tray Times (bowing.)
I am, as you perceive,
And would you of embarrasment relieve.

Saint Thomas.
I thank you, sir—I thank you, on my soul !

Faith. Tray Times.
But you will place yourself 'neath my control ?

Saint Thomas.
You wield an influence which I greatly crave.
And think you can my sinking fortune save.

Faith. Times.
Just so; we *five* can wield a goodly force.
And we will aid you to a proper course.
You must resign—

Saint Thomas (passionately.)
What? Why must I resign?

Faith. Tray Times.
To save yourself from pain—disgrace condign.
Your 'lection was a farce, a travesty;
Your parasites have played deceitfully :
The people do condemn it far and wide,
And all the actors in the scheme deride.
Have you a wish your honor to retain?
Then, throw your office up and run again.
Do this. and you shall have the church's aid.

Saint Thomas.
It shall be done—your wish shall be obeyed.

Faith. Tray Times.
That's right: and now, good sir, here is my hand :
We will obey what e'er you may command.   [*Exit.*

Saint Thomas.
Ha! ha! We'll see! 'Tis well to make pretense:
I'll hold it still, and yet avoid offence.
Illegal got; illegal be resigned,
And hold thy counsel single as thy mind !   [*Exit.*

SCENE III.—*Saint Tom's office—the Saint examining his dedation debits and credits.*

Saint Thomas (looking at a balance sheet.)
'Tis written there—and cannot be denied—
One hundred thousand on the debit side,
In good greenbacks,—commissions, too, beside.
The credit page!—what's in the balance weighed
Against that sum ?   Let's see if I am repaid.
(*Reads.*)—" By one commission as a Senator."
'Tis spurious, not worth a *louis d'or.*
And then, my name, the character I've lost:—
O *precious* whistle, what a price you've cost!
And yet they say I shall not pipe with thee,
Or soothe my anguish with their melody.
Well, now to head them off and play my card,
To hold my office and get their regard.
Yes; I will make pretense that I resign,
Yet keep the office still—securely mine.
My plan to not a single soul I'll tell,—
If I miss heaven, I'll make the most of hell.
[*Enter Methodist Chaplain seeking a Colonelship.*

Chaplain.
Good day, my friend; I hope I find thee well :
Hath aught disastrous to our cause befel ?

Saint Thomas.
Who are you, sir ?   I ne'er saw you before.

Chaplain.
You'll know me ere our conference is o'er !
(*Shows a letter.*)— *Your* letter, sir, in which it is agreed
(Which, pardon me, I do not mean to read.)
That if I will to the Capital go
And cause my brethren to vote so-and-so.
You, in return, have promised unto me
The right and title to a Colonelcy.
I hope you clearly see my drift, or aim—
I've done the work, and come my pay to claim.

Saint Thomas.
But, sir, remonstrances I have received.—
I must deny you, and I'm much agrieved.

Chaplain.
Remonstrances ?   Who dare say aught 'gainst me ?
But, sir. I'll not be haulked by treachery !

I have fulfilled my *promise*—so shall you ;
Or else I'll show you in your colors true !

Saint Thomas.

An officer high in the public 'steem,
Has threatened to divulge our little scheme,
Swears you're unfit a Corporal to be,
And would for aye disgrace a Colonelcy.

Chaplain.

They who affirm this thing of me are few,—
As many hundreds say the same of *you ;*
We're both unfit to fill the place we crave:
But fitness must be buried in the grave,
And sealed beneath the lid of our desires :
'Tis not to *fitness* either one aspires.
Did we but get the which we richly merit,
The which by Nature's laws we *should* inherit,
I fear we both would plod along alone,
Uncalled to rule, uncourted and unknown.
But, *entre nous,* that man has never yet
Refused the place or craft or gold could get.

Saint Thomas.

Now, by my faith, you reason like a sage:
Art fit to be the leader of the Age.
I do intend my office to resign,—
As people say it is not rightly mine,—
But I perhaps shall run me once again,
And so desire your friendship to retain.
If my commands in this you will obey,
I'll make you your commission out straight way.

Chaplain.

Ne're fear for me—I'll be as true as steel ;
More faithful servant ne'er to monarch kneel'd.
[*Saint Tom gives him a commission.*

Saint Thomas.

For many a day for this I'll be abused,
But faithful friends should be right kindly used,
And should I ever your assistance need,
I do believe I'll find a friend indeed

Chaplain.

Depend upon it, sir, I will not fail
To be with you in calm or furious gale.
(*Aside.*)—O, my prophetic soul, no longer doubt !
A Chaplain I came in, a Colonel I go out !   [*Exit*

Saint Thomas.

Nil desperandum ! I will not despair—
Arise, my soul, and cleave the ambient air !
I must be gone to see my Faithful Tray—
His honest smile will drive dull care away.   [*Exit*

SCENE IV.—*Topeka—State Convention in session—St. Thomas discovered on his political death-bed, and Fitz Hindoo and Johan Von Zeitung condoling with him and shedding very affecting tears.*

Saint Thomas.

Weep not, my friends ; this is the way of earth,
Man's life is but a desert waste—a dearth
Of stable joys : a paucity of bliss.
And he is ever striving but to miss
The thing at which he aims.   Would'st thou get good,
Be never ready to do what you would,
But always ready to do what you should.
I was unfit to fill the place I sought,
And bastard schemes are sure to come to naught.

Johannes von Zeitung (in a flood of tears.)
Boo! hoo! Vat shall I do ? Oh! voe is me!
I'll bick up mine traps unt start for Yarmany.
                                    [*Overcome.*

Fitz Hindoo.
Since I've been left so deeply in the lurch,
Boo! hoo! boo! h-o-o! I'll go and join the church!
                              [*Enter Faith. Tray Times,*

Faith. Tray Times (to Tom.)
Good morrow, sir ; your orders were obeyed,
Your resignation I to them conveyed.

Saint Thomas.
Thanks, thanks, my friend ; and how was it received ?

Faith Tray Times.
Such unanimity I ne'r conceived.
Why, sir, the Hall was drown'd with loud applause !
                                    [*Tom dies.*
O, Tom, thy death hath won the great *eclat.*
                              [*Scene closes slowly.*

ACT IV.

SCENE I.—*A political bone-yard.*

Enter Pall-Bearers, with political corpse of ST. THOMAS. FAITH-
TRAY, FITZ HINDOO, JOHAN. VON ZEITUNG *and mourners. Funeral services by* FAITFUL TRAY.

Faith. Tray Times.

Brother Hindoo, please to lead the choir,
And play the fol'wing on your deep toned liar :

Hymn.

Hark ! I hear a deep-toned knell.
　　Hush ! it chimes the notes of death !
Mournful as the last farewell
　　Sighed upon life's parting breath :
Gone, another says each chime,—
Borne beyond the shores of *Time.*

Now another heart is still;
　　Now another voice is mute;
Music can no longer thrill—
　　Lay aside the harp and lute
Nought this sleeping clod can stir—
He shall rest with AARON BURR.

Gathered round that sleeper's bier,
　　Brothers in his day of strife,
Could ye pierce his cold, deaf ear,
　　Would ye call him back to life ?
Would ye bid him rise again ?
Think ye that he sleeps in vain ?

No ! his loss to us is gain ;
　　Good to all his death bestows;
Frees himself from many a pain,
　　Frees our State from future woes—
Tho' his sun in darkness set,
He shall rise more glorious yet.

Oration (by Faith. Tray.)

When great men fall, 'tis right that we should weep,
And all their acts in fond remembrance keep.
In life, 'tis just that we their errors chide :
In death, their every wrong committed hide.
We are but men—of virtues very small,
Disposed to vice as leaves are prone to fall.

Here defunct greatness lies—here virtue sleeps;
Here Mem'ry pauses, views the wreck, and weeps
What recks it whether Death's infernal pangs
Obey the scepter or the serpent's fangs?
Or whether man by calumny be slain,
Or die from "Jersey lightning" on the brain?
Death is an evil clothed in any guise,
And twice an evil, when a great man dies.
Great Thomas, rest thee! Thou hast left a name
Bound with the wreaths of Cæsarean fame!
He, stabbed by Brutus, fell'd him neath the blow.
And thou hast bow'd to an insidious foe.
Thou'rt gone, and we shall mourn for many a day
The fatal stab that stole thy life away.
Kind friend, forgive these tears!—great Cæsar's wounds
Imbue me with a solemn grief profound,
And it is well, that we, his friends, should shed
A tribute tear to Cæsar's memory—dead.
Ambition did not dwell with him alone—
It is a grievous fault we all do own;
And grievously as he hath answered it.
We may ourselves be called to answer it
Great Cæsar sleeps—we, by his death undone,
Siderial orbs without a central sun:
Our cause is lost; we've not an issue left:
Of every hope, political, bereft:
The people cannot read' *John Von Zeitung*.
And *Hindoo's* lyre (liar) is broken and unstrung;
I'm left—poor Faithful Tray—to fight, alone.
Our battles now; our hapless cause bemoan.
But we will bury fallen Cæsar here;
And (well I think I am at least his peer,)
If you should think me worthy of his place,
I'll try to raise our cause from foul disgrace.
But I will stop! I come but to fulfill
These sacred rites, and then to read his will
But first his epitaph to you I'll read.

Epitaph.

Here lies, alas!—no matter who;—
His noble heart beat high and true:
He was a patriot, great and brave,
And gave his life his State to save:
Was brilliant, talented, yet mild,
And gentle as a prattling child;
Respected and beloved by all,
The planet-star of great and small.
—5

No quaint carved slab shall deck thy lowly bed,
To tell thy history to the passer by;
Nor high-wrought monument rear its stately head,
In solemn grandeur, to the azure sky,
To mark the grave where wealth and genius lie.
[*Agitation of the Pall over the bier. Thomas comes to life.*

Saint Thomas.

Ohe Jam satis!—thou infernal dolt!
Thou fool!—thou knave!—thou ape!—thou asses colt!
My resignation is a counterfeit;
I've not resigned—I won't resign a bit!
Some faint—some fall on their knees—some run away in frantic
error, leaving Saint Tom in solemn meditation—"fancy free."

Saint Thomas.

Alone, alone; no friendly voice I hear!—
Hark! How this troubled heart beats wild with fear!
This place so silent, cold, and dark, and drear,
As though grim death himself abideth here.
Come back, oh healthy thought, once more come back,
And Reason's car assume thy wonted track!
What mean these pale habiliments of death
That bind my form and suffocate my breath?
If I be I, why, surely this is I,—
But why these robes of death? When did I die?
Of what disease? Let's see! let's see! let's see!
Oh, reason plays me most deceitfully!
Is there no name to tell the cruel ill
That froze my vital currents 'gainst my will?
Will the vile papers I have left behind,
Assert 'twas aberration of the mind?
Or, growing bolder as they grow more vain,
Affirm I died from fraud upon the brain?
Well, let 'em say't! I scorn the venomed shaft,
I'm now beyond the reach of—Lincoln's draft—
They can but say I met the fatal blade
With a brave heart, that could not be dismayed;
That, living, I was cursed in this alone,
And dying, made its precepts all my own:
And, when, in after years, some knave of State,
Aspiring to be classed among the great,
Shall seek by bribes to compass his desire,
My name shall glow with Caesarean fire,
As he, like those patrician lords of old,
Shall point to me, the daring and the bold,
Who dared to bribe the god of power with gold.
[*Re-enter Faithful Tray Times disguised as a Gipsey woman.*

Faith. Tray Times (*aside.*)
Oh, now, I know that saying is a lie,
That when the brains are out the man will die.
For here is Tom, as brainless a rock.
Yet full of life as is a whipped game cock:
Good morrow, sir; you seem to be in grief:
Command me, sir, if I can give relief.

Saint Thomas (*abstractedly.*)
The heart hath sorrows veil'd from all,
Deep griefs none else can know,
Fierce poignant throbs that crushing fall,
With unresounding blow;
An agony it doth not tell,
(*Dolefully.*)—But hides 'neath smiling mien,
And burning tears from eyes that well,
By other's eyes unseen.

Beneath its secret weight of woe,
Life sinks by slow decay,
And earth no balsam can bestow,
To soothe its weary way ;
In silence groans, in silence sighs,
Nor knows relief from sorrow ;
While hope in siren accents cries—
"Bliss waits thee on the morrow."

But, ah ! that morrow's golden beams
Shine on a broken heart,
And joys are evanescent dreams,
Scarce felt ere they depart ;
And ever thus, from day to day,
Of future bliss we dream
To see each vision swept away,
Adown oblivion's stream.

Oh ! cruel pangs ! oh ! bliss deferred,
Till hope within has died !
Why is the gaunt, grim Chief preferred,
While I am thrust aside ?
Dame Fortune, why on him alone
Thy choicest gifts bestow,
While I am left to sigh and groan
For gems I ne'er may know ?

Faith. Times.
In the expressive lexicon of life,
One word points out our destiny—'tis strife ;

Unceasing strife of will, and toil of brain,
From dawn of life till chaos comes again ;
And he who most expedients can command,
Shall wield that word with high and daring hand ;
Who is most fertile in the art of Vice,
Most fruitful in Conception and Device,
Shall force the gems dame Fortune hath denied,
And mount to power despite of wind and tide.

Saint Thomas.

Too late for me ; I've play'd a double game,
Have tempted Honor with the bribes of Shame !
Drugged by Ambition's foul mephitic speech,
Who told me none my honor could impeach,
Whatever means I might employ to get
This precious pearl on which my soul was set.
I staked a palace 'gainst a living tomb—
I've play'd and lost, and must abide my doom.
(*Abstractedly.*)—There is a serpent famed for beauty rare,
Whose fangs are deadly as its skin is fair,
And—what has given us most complete surprise—
When over-matched, it stings itself and dies :
So doth the subtle serpent base deceit,
By its own acts, ensure its own defeat !

Faith. Tray (*aside.*)

Now, by my faith, his wisdom grows apace,
And the crude gem assumes a brilliant grace,
Ground, shaped and polished by adversity :
The pupil will in time the tutor be ;
The rayless orb my wisdom taught to shine,
Grows with a lustre quite eclipsing mine—
As rain that drops upon a stone for years,
An indentation in the surface wears,
So sparks of knowledge pierce the hardest head,
And make the dunce in time a man well bred.
(*Aloud.*)—You would be free from your determined foe :—
What in return will you on me bestow,
If I shall rid you of this giant, Lane,
And write him on your list of foemen slain ?

Saint Thomas (*despondingly.*)

There is no hope ; I live and yet am dead,
By mine own hand chain'd to dishonor's bed !
Seek not to loose my hands, but let me lie—
Revived again, is but again to die !

Faith. Tray Times.

Despond not, sir; disjointed are the times,
And men may be excused for minor crimes;
Success from mortal sight those crimes shall hide.
'Neath stainless robes, fit for a peerless bride:
Come buckle on your corselet, sword and shield.
And dare once more the fierce politic field:
And you shall win that Senatorial crown—
With robes of splendor, honor and renown.

Saint Thomas

What mean'st thou, woman, by this boastful tale?
I am alone; how can *my* arm prevail
Against the mighty hosts of this dread Chief,
Who hath so often brought my soul to grief?
How knowest thou that, in seeking to obtain
My one desire, I shall not fall again?

Faith. Tray Times,

Whence get the flowers their variegated hues?
Whence come the beams that gild the morning dews?—
'Tis but the reflex of a higher Power,
That gems each drop and tints each brilliant flower
As yon bright sun, from his empyreal throne,
Can robe the dews in lustre all his own,
Can make the gem to shed latent rays,
In fitful flashes or in constant blaze.
So shall the art of which I am possessed,
Force any secret from the Future's breast,
Before the march of Time and Nature's laws
Complete the circuit of effect and cause;—
There is no region whence I may not soar,
No realm so boundless I can not explore.

Saint Thomas.

Go, tell thy idle stories to the wind,
Or to such silly apes as are inclined
To give them credence; I'll no more,—away!
I've been too long of rogues the dupe and prey.

Faith. Tray Times.

What! would'st thou stop to doubt that power of man
Whose mighty grasp the universe can span?
Each orb can measure in the upper skies,
Howe'er remote, and tell its bulk precise?
Can chain the lightning at its dread command?
Can hold the myriad planets in its hand?
And weigh each world as 'twere a grain of sand?

In its research how daring does it climb,
To bask in realms ethereal and sublime!—
All this as truth I know thou dost receive,
Aye, more our schoolmen teach thee to believe.
But I am done;—I come to read thy fate.
And tell thee how thou might be grand and great;
But thou art deaf to wisdom's warning voice,
And I will leave thee to thy foolish choice.

Saint Thomas.

Nay, leave me not; if there is hope for me,
I will embrace the future joyfully,
Will rise again to active, living life,
And court once more the field of bitter strife.

Faith. Tray Times

Enough,—thy path is open straight and plain,
The thing you seek quite easy to obtain.

Saint Thomas.

Point out the course, the measures, and the means.

Faith. Tray Times.

You know a man who bartered pork and beans
For right to sit in yonder stately hall,
That half the nation call the Capitol?
Who, hoping to become a planet star,
Devised a silly "secret circular."
He is unfriendly to your foeman, Lane,
And you must strive his friendship to obtain,
(While still your former friends you must retain.)
And you and he must ply the President
With honey'd phrase and deep-laid argument.
With subtle accusations, false but fair,
Dark innuendoes, like a witch's prayer,
Which when they do assert 'tis a fair day,
"'Tis a very dark night," they plainly say:
Thus while your speech is tuned to friendship's strain,
Let every word a dagger's point contain.

Saint Thomas

I am not gifted in the art of speech,—
You speak of things too far beyond my reach

Faith. Tray Times.

So was not Moses in the days of old,
But Aaron was of crafty speech and bold.

Saint. Thomas.

I'll meet no Aaron, on my mission hence,
To back me with his cunning eloquence.

Faith. Tray Times.

There's Faithful Tray—fast brother to thy soul—
Whose words of fire a nation could control;
He hath been long a worthy friend, well tried,
And will be now a most efficient guide.
One word; you must, on honor bright, resign,
If you your foeman's base would undermine;
And, for the rest, haste to your Faithful Tray—
He will instruct you in the proper way;
Consult him well—in all things him obey.

Saint Thomas.

Again I rise upon an eagle's wings,
To breathe the atmosphere of lords and kings!
O, what I owe thee, woman, who can tell?
But it shall be repaid in full—farewell!

[*Exit Tom.*

Faith. Tray Times.

Ah, Thomas, should I be repaid in full,
I fear thy hands would tear my precious wool,
For while I play thy cards for sake of pelf,
I play to win the golden fleece myself.

[*Exit.*

ACT V.

Scene I.—*Washington—Private apartments of Shoddy Cæsar
Pork-and-Beans—Shoddy Cæsar and his Secretary discovered.*

S. C. P.

This "circular," to use a patent phrase,
Is like the Bull against the Comet's blaze,
Well written, as its purpose is well meant,
But shows its author's intellect mis-spent.

Secretary.

Your pardon, sir; I wrote it in your pay—
And being paid, 'tis not all thrown away.

S. C. P.

True, true, my friend; but I who paid the score
Have squandered money shall return no more;—
I blame you not—I am myself to blame:
I hoped through this to win a statesman's name,
And when I thought myself with honors crown'd,
Alas! in sack-cloth, I must kiss the ground!
Thus, seeking honor in a jesuit's guise
I've won his hateful name, but lost his prize.

Secretary.

What would'st thou be? The leader of the train
Of corrupt minds who pander to the vain,
Delusive idol, Evanescent Power,
By tenure held that's broken in an hour?

S. C. P.

That is the obnoxious feature in our laws,
Of crimes politic great, first parent cause:
We're gilded butterflies—ephemera,
Seen but a moment ere we pass away,
Pull'd from our peers, and o'er betters placed,
To rule awhile and then to be displaced—
To melt away into the plebian herd,
With our patrician caste? Why, that's absurd!

Secretary.

There was a time, (*but very long ago,*)
When politicians were as chaste as snow;
No scheming then, no tricks and turns abrupt,
Nor gold could buy, nor lust of power corrupt.
Men sought not office—office sought its men,
Who sought the sweets of private life again;
Thus, living—honored for their virtues rare,
In death, revered for living lives so fair.
Go learn from them—those giant men of yore—
Repent, and follow them, and sin no more.   [*Exit*

S. C. P.

How very strange—incredible!—it seems
But a mere fancy of the Poet's dreams,
That man the acme step of power should shun,
And yield to other's what he fairly won;—
It is a virtue past my fartherest ken,
And surely not possessed by modern men.
Who gets an office, gets it by deceit;
To hold it—he must learn to lie and cheat!
Tis well for me in these I am *au fait;*

For all mankind are nought but beasts of prey;
Recherché in all they openly enact,
In intercourse, fastidious and exact;
To fawn and flatter is their daily trade,
While scheming how the fawn'd may be betrayed;—
The game of life is intricate, abstruse,
Plain, honest dealing is of little use;
The more adept the larger prizes win——

Saint Thomas (entering.)
And Shoddy Cæsar can't be taken in:—
Good morrow, Cæsar; I congratulate
My first of Statesmen, and my foeman's mate.

S. C. P.
Bonjour, Monsieur, Saint Thomas, bon et cher.—
What thing important brings Saint Thomas here?
Seekest thou a draw, sir, at the public teat?
To batten on the price of base deceit?

Saint Thomas.
Thou'rt merry, sir;—an honest place I seek,
And on that purpose come I here to speak.

S. C. P.
O, very true,—an honest *place* no doubt,—
All men are honest—till they are found out.

Saint Thomas.
Why, Cæsar, thou'rt a man of pleasant wit
Whose sharpest arrows tickle where they hit;
Keen-edged, sharp-pointed, thrown with skill profound,
And soothe their victims while they deeply wound.

S. C. P.
There's not an office-seeker in this place,
But wears an honest, sanctimonious face,
Talks loudly of his virtues, small and great,
Swears he but seeks the welfare of his State—
Who, were he but in earnest when he speaks,
Should hang himself, to gain the point he seeks;
With words a mile in length, but meaningless,
Harps on his patriotic nobleness,
Grows eloquent as he his love portrays,
And does not comprehend the half he says,—
Because, forsooth! his second-handed speech
Contains a wisdom far beyond his reach.

—6

Saint Thomas.

Well, Cæsar, I no boughten speech have brought,—
I scorn the use of second-handed thought!

S. C. P.

Thou art at fault, sir, sadly indiscreet,—
None of thine *own* nor *other's* to repeat;
'Twere better, sir, another's be employed,
Than you of thought entirely be devoid.

Saint T homas.

Thy wit hurts deeper as it older grows,
As do the corns that twinge our tender toes.

S. C. P.

Good sense grows brighter as it older grows,
As does the blossom on our precious nose.

Saint Thomas.

So, ho! our nose stands out in bold relief,
And proves our——

S. C. P.

Mouth to be an arrant thief.

Saint Thomas.

Now, if the body of thy sparkling wit
Be equal to these drops that sample it,
'Twere better you uncork the whole at once.

S. C. P.

Nay, sparing deal good wine unto a dunce;
for, (be't to Nature's honor or disgrace,)
Wine seeks the most convenient empty place,
And dunce's stomachs being always full,
It seeks a lodging in the brainless skull.

Saint Thomas.

Nay, I will stomach thy whole stock of wine,
And in the bottom of the cask will dine,
And desert on its lowest depth of lees—
Though pork and beans should make the whole of these.

S. C. P.

Upon my faith, that is a good retort,
And handled nicely as a last resort,
And by its deeply wounding thrust we'll quit
This fierce encounter useless of our wit,
And fall to something of more serious mood;
'or wine is best partook with solid food,—

And as you have a purpose to fulfill,
Let's to that purpose with a right good will.

Saint Thomas.

Just so; that strikes me in the proper place,
And I must thank you for your courtly grace;
E'en as your wit superior is to mine,
So doth your wisdom glow with light divine;
And wit and wisdom in one head combined,
Complete the invoice of a giant mind,
Which shows the value of its stock in trade,
In solving problems dark and deeply laid,
And I such problem have brought here to solve,
In hope that you the answer might evolve.

S. C. P.

Take one from two, what answer doth remain ?
Substract—Who shall it be? thyself? or, Lane?
Two shall be grinding in the mill, you know.
And——

Saint Thomas.

I would stay and let this other go!
The last shall be first: so says the Book,—
Let me remain—and be the other took.

S. C. P.

Why, let the people in their right decide
Who shall be taken and who shall abide.

Saint Thomas.

Did I but hold the reins, 'twere *apropos*,—
But drifting with them I might drift too slow.

S. C. P.

Who can not lead the van of meaner things
Will never win the fellowship of kings;
Who would be great must on himself depend;
For—to be plain with you, my right good friend—
Man lends his fellow no efficient aid,
But where there's surety it will be repaid ;—
We are by nature selfish in our schemes,
And always first in Fancy's golden dreams:
Our fellows are our adjuncts, used at will,
Or thrown aside,—our purpose to fulfill,—
Just as the well bred scholar times his lore
To please the courtier, or the country boor ;
Assumes the rustic, or a polished grace,
To suit the times, the manners, and the place :

Here is the key to power's close guarded gate—
Who can't command, must e'en conciliate.

Saint Thomas.

On that same subject came I hear to speak;
For that same purpose thy assistance seek;
Soliciting that, in my interview,
What I affirm, shall be referred to you,
And you, with many a fine paid compliment.
Return this answer to the President,
That—" *What he says is truth, beyond a doubt;* "
And thus, you see, we'll work the problem out.

S. C. P.

I've lost my prestige here—I'm not at par:
That Schofield, and my secret circular,
Have thrown my grist of sand in mine own eyes,
And caused my fall—where I had hoped to rise.
But I will introduce you, that you may
Work out your problem in some other way.

Saint Thomas.

Thanks, thanks, my friend !—if we but get it through.
I'll share its fairest honors fair with you.

S. C. P.

O, hang the honors—they are negative!
Men on the profits, not the honors, live;
But we must risk,—no risk, no hope to win!
And men are oft " put out " when " taken in !"

[*Exit*

Scene II.—*Executive Mansion, Washington—Mr. President and St. Tom discovered.*

Saint Thomas.

And now, your excellency,—to be brief,—
This Senator, this grim and mighty chief,
Hath,—with his wicked wiles and cunning arts,—
Against my wishes, stolen the people's hearts;
And I—who fear him, in his presence cower—
Have come to you to rid me of his power!

Mr. President.

Why, that reminds me of an anecdote :—
A boy once, traveling on a Western boat,
Let fall an apple in the river's tide,
And to the Captain hastily applied—

" O, Captain, stop your craft—dear Captain, do !
My apple's overboard—boo, hoo ! boo, hoo !"

Saint Thomas.
And, now, when I have fairly bought his place,
He laughs and says—" Be not in too much haste ; "
That when the proper time arrives that he
His will should make—he'll kindly think of *me !*

Mr. President.
Another story : In a country fair,
A monarch had a most unnatural heir,
Who, chiding tardy nature's long delay
To crown the son, and take the sire away,
Resolved that he would aid old father Time,
(Which, in the laws of Nature, is a crime,)
And by some swifter means the prize compel—
But, lo ! the son, and *not* the father, fell !
" Go slow," St. Thomas, is the moral here :
For haste oft hastens what we most do fear !

Saint Thomas.
And thou, (I think it scurvy, too, of thee,)
Clothest him with power thou should'st bestow on me ;
And I must yield to him in my own State,
Where—by the laws—I have nor peer nor mate !

Mr. President
Possessed of large estates in Illinois,
A farmer lived who had two growing boys,
And knowing the capacity of each,
That one had skill beyond the other's reach,
He placed such " portions " 'neath each lad's control,
As would enhance the value of the whole :
But now the weaker—of perverted will—
Was jealous of his brother's better skill,
And, goaded by his passion's 'vengeful fire,
To kill his brother was his chief desire :
Yet could he not accomplish this alone—
His purpose being to his brother known,
So he resolved to get his father's aid,
(Could he by false coined charges be betrayed ;)
The father, wishing to allay the force
Of his son's hatred took a middle course ;
From him who had the most he took away,
And gave the other, till an equal weigh
Of power belonged to both, when—strange to say—
Both brothers were incensed ; and from that day

The three became involved in bitter strife,
Which ended only with the end of life.
The father said, once, (telling this to me :)
" *Part not two friends in hopes of making three !* "

Saint Thomas.
So you refuse to rid me of my foe ?
Then, I am done,—Oh ! whither shall I go ?

Mr. President.
A darkey stumbled on a skunk one day,
Which threw its liquid fire and rushed away;
The darkey sneezing—" Golly, what a smell,"
Threw off his coat and darted off, pell-mell,
After the e'er-perfumed aristocrat,
Swearing—" Ef I cotch dat ar pole'm cat
I'll show him I's a gemlan, I'll be bound ! "
But, lo ! the pole-cat dodged into the ground.
But what is queer in what I meant to say,
No hole was found where he had hid away.

Saint Thomas.
Why, how could this be so, I'd like to know ?   No hole
    was found ?

Mr. President.
No hole, St. Tom—Go slow ;
Who " hastens slowly " often travel fast.

Saint Thomas.
Well, what was his conclusion at the last ?

Mr. President.
He pondered deeply, scratched his woolly head,
Until he found the labyrinthian thread ;
'Twas this, that—" Dat ar 'fernal catempole.
Had fust gone in, and den pulled in his hole ! "
        [*St. Tom takes the hint, hunts his hole, and scene closes.*

*Scene III.—St. Tom in a fit of abstraction has subtracted him-
self from the vile dust of the Central City, and wandered for into
the mazy labyrinths of the wilderness of (Sam) Cottonwood and
(Fernandy) Bass-wood, and is musing over the withered flower
of his defunct Virtue*

Saint Thomas.
Sweet flower ! upon this lonely wild,
Where Desolation's sway

Hath mar'd the works of human pride,
And broods o'er their decay,
What freak of Nature placed thee here
'Neath plebian weeds to dwell,
Hid from yon glorious Source of Light,
Secure as monk in cell?

Art thou—like me—a stranger here,
Exotic to the soil;
Once fondly pruned by maiden hands
That knew no other toil?
Or did'st thou bloom indiginous,
At Nature's dread command,—
Unseen before by mortal eye,
Untouched by mortal hand?

Thou hast a hist'ry—so have I!
But thine thou can'st not tell,
And mine—for lack of man to hear—
Remains untold as well!
O! had'st thou but a living voice,
I'd bind thee on my heart,
We'd roam companions of these wilds,
And never more would part.

'Tis hard that I should languish here,
On this bleak, desert shore,
Thrust out from dear companionship
That I shall know no more!
But, while I grieve, 'tis sweet to think
Earth dwells not all in gloom;
She still retains some verdant spot
Where flowers do ever bloom!

Though from my eyes, in sable night
Yon sun may melt away,
For her he shines eternally—
To her 'tis always day:
Though robed her Poles in ice and frost,
Some spot there is where Spring
Breathes incense on the balmy air,
And birds continual sing.

" L. D." in Nature's thrilling book
Are stamp'd on every page;
They dwell throughout God's Universe,
They run through every Age:

Light blent with Darkness, Life with Death,
Enduring as the Sky;—
Whom Nature's laws bring into life,
By Nature's laws—must die!

Even as I crush thy petals now
I spoil thy beauty's bloom ;
But, dying, thou for gratitude,
Send'st back a sweet perfume ;
Distilling odor on the hand
That snaps life's golden thread,
As if—"That blow hath given me bliss,"
Thy passing spirit said.

Thus dies the martyr for the right,
Thus doth the good man fall ;
His life a round of benefits—
Death crowns them glorious—all !

*Enter Fernandy, robed in the insignia of a cardinal of the Knights
of Liberty, and branded on the forehead : " Property of J. D.—
C. S. A."*

Fernandy

Who art thou, sir, so daring, rash and rude,
As on my realms thus boldly to intrude ?

Saint Thomas.

Your pardon, noble sir ; I do not know
The thing I am, or whither I should go.

Fernandy.

Why, thou art like a wrecked and shroudless bark,
Without a rudder—drifting in the dark.
What wast thou ere thou camest to this estate ?
Come, speak the truth, nor aught extenuate !

Saint Thomas.

How came I here ? What sort of man was I ?
In former years. (the truth I'll not deny !)
I was—ha ! ha !—to answer you quite pat—
A kind of hybrid—'twixt a fox and cat,
Or fish and flesh—a Calhoun dimmycrat.

Fernandy.

A rebel angel, who has bartered creed
For transient power ? A dimmycrat, indeed !
Base renegade ! What punishment is due
To politicians recreant as you ?

Bow down to dust, then base and low-bred cur,
And kiss my feet! Nor shalt thou rise nor stir
Till thou hast done this penance for thy crime,
And promised better for the coming time!

Saint Thomas (kissing Fernandy's toe.)
Behold, the dog his vomit seeks once more,
The sow her mire—as she was wont of yore.
Let me return—my heinous sin forgive:
For lo! 'tis sweet in *unity* to live.

Fernandy
Now, by my holy hat and robes of state,
That smacks too much of abolition prate!
'Tis peace we want—not *unity*—thou dunce!
Cry " *Peace!* " or I will cleave thy brain at once'

Saint Thomas.
Indeed, my lord, thy threats are all in vain—
My fane of reason is bereft of brain.
But " *Peace* " I cry and echo it again.

Fernandy.
Wilt thou once more unto our faith return?

Saint Thomas.
I will, my lord; it is for that I yearn.

Fernandy.
Enough; I seal thee with our sacred seal,
[*Brands Tom in the forehead:* " *Property of J. D.—C. S. A.*'
Thou'rt ours again. for woe as well as weal!

Saint Thomas (rising.)
Thanks, thanks, my lord; but now what shall I do,
To prove how constant I can be and true?

Fernandy.
Return at once unto your Sovereign State,
And gambol with your former defunct mates,
Who, four long years, have lain with bated breath,
A living carcass in the house of death!
There is a *Gambler* there. one *Willard Stone*—
As *Peter* is a rock, by scripture shown—
He and my brother swine-herd Cotton-wood
Have made arrangements for your mutual good.

Saint Thomas.
Thy good advice I hasten to obey—
With such a guide I cannot miss my way

—7

Let Lincoln's dogs along my pathway howl—
I'll fool 'em yet, or doff my saintly cowl.   [*Exit*

SCENE IV.—*Abode of the Seeress Madame Draskowski; Jug*
hustle-proclamation Lager-beer McDown-on-Sunday laws, with a
jug and mug of his official beverage discovered.

Sings.

O, lager beer, I love thee dear;
For thou elected'st me;
And I have caused our " Sunday Laws "
To let thee travel free.

So, now, we're quits:—like two gay wits,
With rival repartee,
We've tussel'd long, we've tusseled strong—
Henceforth we'll brothers be!

I'm in the lurch; for, lo, the church
Is down on lager beer;
But let them pray—I'll drink and bray,
Nor once their censure fear.

I've got their votes, and turned coats
Oft look as well as new;
Or black, or white, or purple bright,
May wear as long as blue.   [*Drinks*

Long life to lager—making single double;
The fount of joy and bane of every trouble;
Vive le lager—death to *eau de vie*—
The church shall yield to lager beer and me.

[*Enter Madame Draskowski.*

Mad. D.
Bon soir, mon cher Monsieur; Me cherchez vous?

J. L. McD.
Parlez vous—nix cum rouse—I think I do.

Mad. D.
Quel voulez vous? Es tu in cul de sac?

J. L. McD.
Ich nix feestay—mein nome is " Lager Mac."

Mad. D.
Whas wilch tu hov? Bien l'allemand vouz speak?

J. L. McD.
Pray Madame, is that Latin, Celt, or Greek ?

Mad. D.
Does Monsieur Lager want his fortune told ?

J. L. McD.
Not I.   I've come to buy, not to be sold.

Mad. D.
Tres bien, *Monsieur, il est le* same to me,
Or I sell thee, or I am sold to thee :
My trade is interdicted as a vice,
And I must ply it for a goodly price ;
For gold in pocket and a cheek of brass.
Will set man's impress on an ape or ass.

J. L. McD.
Here is a fee, your service to retain :   [*Gives money.*
When that is done, I'll make it good again.

Mad. D.
Thanks, thanks, Monsieur !   I have a magic stone,
Could make its owner mistress of a throne,
A common pebble, by its outer look,
But, lo ! the index to the Future's book—
That points ahead thro' each succeeding Age,
To the *denouncement* of each thrilling page.

J. L. McD.
No better real than isthe counterfeit,
As wisdom often is ensnared by wit,—
And as the false full well will answer me.
I'll swear 'tis genuine as a stone can be ;
For be it false or genuine matters not,
If you will give the cue and guide the plot,—
I wrote a letter some few weeks ago,
In hopes that I might prove the overthrow
Of party power, and make myself to reign
In Carney's stead—and in despite of Lane.
Meet me to-night—our plans we will arrange
With deep deceptions and devices strange ;—
E'en as the witch of Endor is renown'd,
Who called to life the prophet from the ground,
So shall the fame thy skill shall win to-night,
Glow with a fervent and undying light.

Mad. D.
Enough !   I will be there,—till then, farewell ;
Or false or true, I'll work a magic spell.   [*Exeunt*

SCENE V.—" *Council Chamber*" *of the Witches of Bolterdom—*
very dark.

Enter FAITHFUL TRAY *in the guise of* "*first witch*," *meeting* JO-
HAN. VON ZEITUNG.

Johan. Von Zeitung.

Brother, why this sister's dress ?

First Witch.

Brother, we are in distress,
And sweet Hecate's aid would press.
Haste and don thy robes—away !   [*Exit Von Zeitung*
As the night doth hide the day,
Veiling deeds from mortal eye,
We detection may defy,
Neath these robes and in the gloom
Of our secret "Council Room."

[*Enter Fitz Hindoo as* "*second witch.*"

Sister, hail !   The cauldron sings :
On its steamy, vapor wings,
Spirits red, and spirits white,
Spirits grey, and black as night,
Spirits in confusion jam'd,
Spirits by the still-house dam'd,
And in hell's deep dungeons cram'd;
Traitor spirits, once of earth ;
Traitors still, in second birth—
Beings here and there of shame—
Mount on rills of sulph'rous flame,
O'er the land they have betrayed
To the Chieftain of the spade,
Who, to save our foeman's slaves,
Digs our patriot freemen's graves ;
And if we would win his aid,
We, with him, must ply the spade.

Second Witch.

Sister, I am ready, quite—
Armed and harnessed for the fight;
So the work is plan'd and *paid,*
I shall shun nor Peace nor Spade—
Tho' the Union be betrayed ;
This for place, and that for gold—
Man is ever bought and sold.

[*Scene opens back, disclosing inner Pandemonium.   Cauldron in*
center, and a lot of beer barrels, emptied at the last election, back
center

Enter Singing Witches, Col. Quack, Cotton-Wood *and* Sheepy

Sisters, hail!   Our dread alarms
Fall beneath the potent charms ;—
Here are two commissions got
In the Senatorial plot ;
Thomas dead and off the track,
These shall cook for Lager Mac.

[*Throws them in Cauldron*

Enter Johan. Von Bittung *as* " *Third Witch.*"

Third Witch.

"Sunday Laws" shall bubble here,
For the prince of lager beer ;
Hoofs of mule and ears of ass,
Eat upon the mountain pass,
In the cauldron smoke with wrath,
Till John finds his long lost Path.

[*Throws them in*

First Witch.

Spades are trumps, and here's the jack,
Photograph of little Mac ;
Here's Jeff. Davis' coat of mail,
Rent in twain by Lincoln's rail ;
You, whose master brought us trouble,
Shall for Peace McClellan bubble.

[*Throws them in.*

Sisters, form the charmed ring—
Round the cauldron dance and sing.

[*All dance and sing*

Thus we labor, hand-in-hand,
Guardians of our slave-cursed land ;
This for woe, and that for weal ;
Spirits, from the vapor smoke,
Aid us in this master stroke—
Triumph to our eyes reveal !

Second Witch.

Hark ! I hear our Tom Cat mew !

Third Witch.

I the click of Steel-trap, too.

First Witch.

Let them come, the game is done—
Spades and lager beer have won !

Enter Saint Thomas.

Saint Thomas

Beldames bold, perverse and saucy crew !
What subtle purpose came ye here to do ?
Know ye not an agent I have sent
To treat with our prospective President ?

Enter TOMMY C. STEEL-TRAP.

Brother, tell us of the fight,
What its signs of promise are?"

T. C. S.

Brother, wrong has conquer'd right—
They will not receive you there!

Saint Thomas.

Brother, this is painful news—
Lo! it cleaves my heart in twain!

First Witch.

Brother, why do they refuse
To receive the Saint again?

T. C. S.

Tom so oft his coat hath changed,
That they think he is deranged;
Now a " coon," and now a "cat "—
Whig and old line democrat;
Any thing for power and pelf,
Little you and big myself;
When you think he will—he won't,
Now you have him, now you don't;
Unsolved freak of Nature's laws,
Fitted but to damn a cause;—
So they dare not take him back,
Lest he throw them off' the track,
Bringing ruin on the whole—
Killing body, blasting soul!—
Thus they say and thus advise—
" Tom would show himself more wise,
And a handsome competence might earn,
If to bacon contracts he'd return."

Saint Thomas.

" This is the most unkindest cut of all "—
To stab, and smile to see their victim fall!
Oh! could the awful tomb to me unclose,
As when it answered Endor's magic lyre,
Where, from the quaking earth, the prophet rose.
And hurled on wicked Saul his furious ire,
'n barbed arrows tipped with words of fire,
And doomed him swiftly to death's dread repose
Then might my boyhood's idol rise once more,
And ope' for me the Future's mystic door!

Second Witch.

Brother, tell us, who is this
Could reveal thy woe or bliss?

Saint 'Thomas.

He the terror once of coons,
John, surnamed the great Calhoun.

Enter MADAME DRASKOUSKI

Mad. D.

Be thy fondest wish fulfill'd ;—
Here is power so deeply skill'd,   [*Exhibits magic pebble.*
That the viewless spirit land
Yields its gems when I command !—
Empress of the nether world,
Where the great unwash'd are hurl'd,
Democrats renown'd of State,
Bodiless, do congregate ;
Living—false to man and God,
Dying—laid beneath the sod
All of value they could claim—
Steep'd their names in endless shame ;
By the seething cauldron's light,
Hie thee to the earth to-night.

[*J. L. McD.*, *in the guise of Hecate, rises out of an empty lager beer cask.*

Hecate.

Sorceress with magic stone,
Mistress of my art and throne,
Queen of all our bearded band,
I am here at thy command :
Speak—I hasten to obey !
Tell thy wish—I am away !

Mad. D.

Goddess of the wind and storm,
Send to earth, in living form,
Him who struck the first fell blow
For the UNION's overthrow !

[*Hecate descends.*

Voice (under ground.)

Hela, open wide thy gate,
Mortals anxiously await—
Spirit, go and read their fate !

J. Lager Mac rises again as Calhoun.

Why my body from its sleep,
Why my soul from Hades' deep,
Call ye back to earthly life,
Where the waves of angry strife—
Fires ignited by my hand—
Desolate our Fatherland ?
Thomas, ere to-morrow's sun,

Blasted are thy hopes—undone;
Thou—thy fraud, thy deepest plot,
Shall be buried and forgot.
Sad, indeed, will be thy fall;
For no tears shall drown thy pall,
And with me, accursed in name,
Shall thou rest—a thing of shame,
Beldames, haste; prepare the bier,—
Wove's the web for lager beer;
Strong's the woof, and fine the thread,
Spun from entrails of the dead,
By the goddess of the Fates:
Hela, close again thy gates!   [*Descends.*

    Saint Thomas (to his recreant confreres.)
  Deceitful wretches—false as false can be—
Your double-dealing quite hath vanquished me!
Ye lying children of the god of lies—
Ye hideous monsters in a human guise—
Who mock at honor, justice, truth and right;
Whose presence doth insult, disgust the sight;—
Ye bastard issue of his traitor hand,
Formed to make desolate a smiling land,
To blast a country in its vernal morn;
And crush the hopes of millions yet unborn;
Your touch is poison, your infectious breath
Is frought with ruin, devastation—death!
Confusion on your footsteps wait,
Disease, despair and scowling hate.
Around your forms their horrid mantles fling,
And conscience wound you with relentless sting!
May war o'erwhelm ye with a crimson wave,
Nor Mercy stretch to ye her hand to save!
The Nation's curse, the Nation's shame,
With furies' flight may ye be hurl'd
Down, down to your native world,
To fan and feed its flame.   [*Tom dies.*

    Enter J. L. McD. and pall bearers.
       J. L. McD.
  My native world is where thine office shines;
To-morrow's sun shall see that office mine.
   [*Grand funeral and triumphal procession. Pall bearers carry St. Tom's "cold corpse" on a bier. Witches carry J. L. McD. astride a keg of lager, and we drop the curtain, hoping that the next Administration may prove to be a good egg.*